Who Will Play With Me ?

For Anna Bootle

BLACKIE CHILDREN'S BOOKS
Published by the Penguin Group
Penguin Books Ltd, 27 Wrights Lane, London W8 5TZ, England
Penguin Books Australia Ltd, Ringwood, Victoria, Australia
Penguin Books Canada Ltd, 10 Alcorn Avenue, Toronto, Ontario, Canada M4V 3B2
Penguin Books (NZ) Ltd, 182 – 190 Wairau Road, Auckland 10, New Zealand

Penguin Books Ltd, Registered Offices: Harmondsworth, Middlesex, England

First published 1992
1 3 5 7 9 10 8 6 4 2

Text and illustrations copyright© Michele Coxon, 1992

The moral right of the author/illustrator has been asserted

A CIP catalogue record for this book is available from the British Library
ISBN 0 216 93213 0

First American edition published 1992 by
Peter Bedrick Books, 2112 Broadway, New York, NY 10023

Library of Congress Cataloging-in-Publication Data is available for this title
ISBN 0 87226 469 6

Printed in Hong Kong

Who Will Play With Me ?

Michele Coxon

Blackie
London

Bedrick / Blackie
New York

Pumpkin had a lovely home.
She had a warm soft bed and plenty of toys.
But she was lonely.
'Who will play with me?'

'Will you play with me?'
'No,' yawned Captain, the old cat.
'I want to sleep and dream of fish.'

'Will you play with me?'
Pumpkin asked the lady.
'Ouch, no!' she cried.
'I'm busy, go outside and play.'

'Will you play with me?'
 the kitten asked the birds.
'No,' sang the birds.
'We must find food to eat.'
And they flew off leaving only a feather behind.

Pumpkin crawled through the jungle of the grass

and came whiskers to nose with a funny creature.
It had two big green eyes and a furry head.
'Will you play with me?'

Turn the page and see who will play with Pumpkin.
Then close the book, turn it upside-down, and start
again from the other end!

and came nose to whiskers with a funny creature.
It had two big green eyes, a pink nose and a furry face.

'Will you play with me?'

Turn the page and see who will play with Luke.
Then close the book, turn it upside-down, and start
again from the other end!

Luke crawled through the jungle of the grass

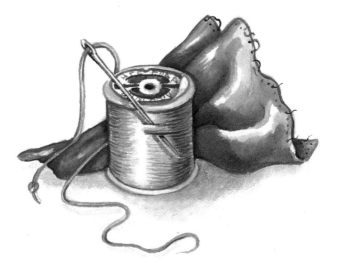

'Will you play with me?'
the boy asked a frog.
'No,' croaked the frog.
'I must find some food to eat.'
and he hopped off leaving only a wet puddle.

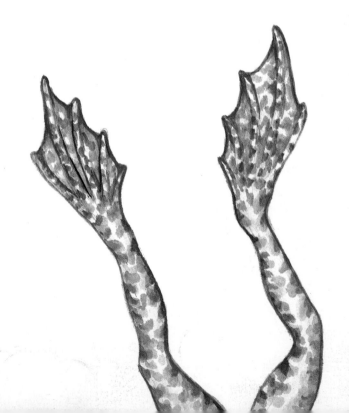

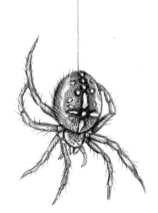

'Will you play with me?'
Luke asked his mum.
'No!' she cried.
'I'm busy, go outside and play.'

'Will you play with me?'
'No,' yawned Ben, the old dog.
'I want to sleep and dream of bones.'

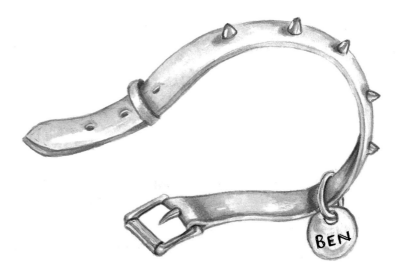

Luke had a lovely home.
He had a warm soft bed and plenty of toys.
But he was lonely.
'Who will play with me?'

Who Will Play With Me ?

Michele Coxon

Blackie
London

Bedrick / Blackie
New York

For Anna Bootle

BLACKIE CHILDREN'S BOOKS
Published by the Penguin Group
Penguin Books Ltd, 27 Wrights Lane, London W8 5TZ, England
Penguin Books Australia Ltd, Ringwood, Victoria, Australia
Penguin Books Canada Ltd, 10 Alcorn Avenue, Toronto, Ontario, Canada M4V 3B2
Penguin Books (NZ) Ltd, 182 – 190 Wairau Road, Auckland 10, New Zealand

Penguin Books Ltd, Registered Offices: Harmondsworth, Middlesex, England

First published 1992
1 3 5 7 9 10 8 6 4 2

A CIP catalogue record for this book is available from the British Library
ISBN 0 216 93213 0

First American edition published 1992 by
Peter Bedrick Books, 2112 Broadway, New York, NY 10023

Library of Congress Cataloging-in-Publication Data is available for this title
ISBN 0 87226 469 6

Printed in Hong Kong